ERIKA MCGANN grew up in Drogheda and now lives in Dublin. As a kid she wanted to be a witch, but was no good at it, so now she spends her time writing supernatural stories, and living vicariously through her characters. She hopes, in time, to develop the skills to become an all-powerful being. She has written three other books about Grace and her friends, *The Demon Notebook*, *The Broken Spell* and *The Watching Wood*.

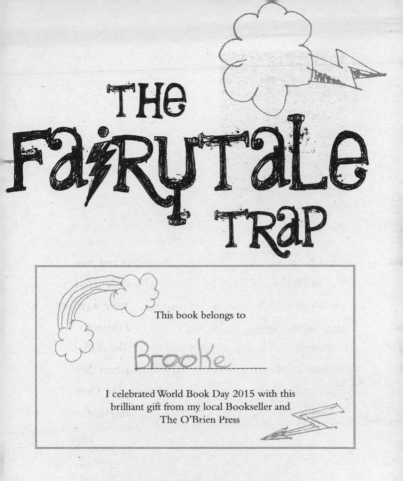

THE FAIRYTALE TRAP

This book belongs to

Brooke

I celebrated World Book Day 2015 with this
brilliant gift from my local Bookseller and
The O'Brien Press

**Winner of the Waverton Good Read
Children's Award 2014**

ERIKA McGANN

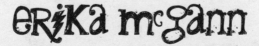

THE O'BRIEN PRESS
DUBLIN

First published 2015 by The O'Brien Press Ltd.,
12 Terenure Road East, Rathgar, Dublin 6, Ireland.
Tel: +353 1 4923333; Fax: +353 1 4922777
E-mail: books@obrien.ie
Website: www.obrien.ie

ISBN: 978-1-84717-725-4

10 9 8 7 6 5 4 3 2 1
19 18 17 16 15

Layout and design: The O'Brien Press Ltd.
Cover and internal illustrations by Emma Byrne
Printed and bound by CPI Group (UK) Ltd, Croydon, CR0 4YY

The paper in this book is produced using pulp from
managed forests.

The O'Brien Press receives financial assistance from

FOR MARY,

WHO ALWAYS LOVED A GOOD STORY.

conTenTs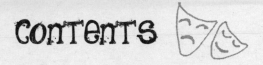

1

a walrus impression

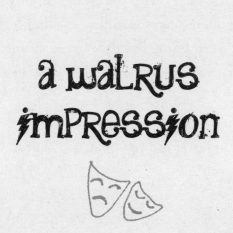

In a dark room, in a dark closet, inside a dark trunk was a soft, cloth cap. It lay between layers of ordinary clothes, but it was no ordinary cap. Kings and queens had worn it, gypsies and paupers too. Armies had fought over it and people had died for it, and many longed to have it. But no-one ever really owned this cap, not really. The cap belonged to nobody but itself. It moved from person to person. It did this because it was always bored. People were so *boring*. And the cap hated being bored. So it left each owner and searched for something interesting, something exciting; a really good story. Inside this dark trunk, in this dark closet, in this dark room…the cap waited.

✳✳✳

'Okay, Grace, and now you're a walrus. Give me a walrus!'

Grace half-crouched and swayed from side to side in what, she hoped, was a decent imitation of a walrus. She could feel her cheeks burning as Andrew Wallace snickered from the back of the drama class.

'More. More walrus!' Mr Dogberry's apple-cheeked face was redder than hers, though from exertion rather than embarrassment in his case. 'And now you're a sunflower, reaching for the sun. Reach, reach for that glorious sun!'

Grace stretched her arms to the ceiling. She wished she could simply use her magic skills to conjure up a sunflower, if he wanted one so badly. But witchcraft at school? Out of the question.

'Come on!' Mr Dogberry's orange-tinted spectacles bounced on his nose as he jumped up and down with enthusiasm. 'That sun is your life force, you're a sunflower. Now reach! Reach for the sun!'

Grace went up on her tiptoes, but her shirt was pulling out of her waistband. She wobbled as she waved one hand up while trying to tuck her shirt tail under her jumper with the other.

'Alright, you can relax. Good effort...I guess.' The drama teacher's flat tone revealed what he really thought, but Grace didn't care. She rushed to her seat, relieved that the excruciating spectacle was over.

'Una, you're up.'

Una shot to her feet, and immediately struck

the pose of a springing tiger. She squinted her grey eyes, and her pretty, elfin features became those of a cat on the hunt. On command she became a broken ladder, her short black, bob hanging to one side. Even her impression of a carton of apple juice was convincing.

This wasn't what Grace had expected when she signed up for the school drama group with Una and Rachel. She had thought they'd be reciting Shakespeare monologues, not pretending to be flowers and juice cartons. She watched Una balance on one leg and beep like a traffic light. If this was acting, Grace decided, then an actor had to be totally immune to embarrassment. And she was definitely not immune.

Rachel was her usual elegant self when her turn came around. With layers of shimmering, chestnut hair and porcelain skin, she looked every bit the theatre star as she deftly worked her way through Mr Dogberry's list of improbable objects. When her go was over, she dropped into the chair beside Grace and winked. They both knew they could have conjured up any number of unlikely objects for their teacher – but this, of course, was a secret.

'Sir,' she said, 'are we going to find out about the show today?'

'Well, since you're all so eager to know,' Mr Dogberry smirked, 'I can indeed reveal the details of our upcoming performance. This year's school pantomime will be my own interpretation of that very great fairytale, *Red Riding Hood.*'

There was some disappointed mumbling.

'A *fairytale?*' said Andrew Wallace. 'That's so lame. Can we not do something cooler than that?'

The teacher's face pinched like he was sucking a lemon.

'Mr Wallace, I think you'll find that my vision, which explores the darker themes of the original story, will be far more than a...' he waggled his plump fingers in the air to make exaggerated quote marks, '…"lame" fairytale. In *my* version, the young Red Riding Hood is devoured by the wolf and, instead of being rescued by the huntsman, never again sees the light of day.'

'Cheerful,' muttered Grace.

Andrew raised an eyebrow, but looked unconvinced.

'I was wondering,' the teacher went on smoothly, 'if your menacing demeanour could lend itself well to the *central* role of the Big Bad Wolf. But if you feel the story has no merit, then—'

'No, no, sir!' Andrew interrupted. 'Sounds good, sir. Brilliant!'

'Excellent.' Mr Dogberry's eyes squinted under his spectacles and he carefully unfolded a sheet of paper. 'And now I can announce the rest of the castings. Everybody listening?'

✷✷✷

'Servant number two?' Grace plopped into a chair in the lunchroom. 'I knew I'd get a rubbish part. Just 'cos I can't be a walrus on command.'

'Aw, I'm sorry.' Adie was sitting at the other end of the table, going though a new spell book she and Delilah had found in the local magic shop, but when she saw Grace's disappointed face she moved next to her and gave her arm a squeeze. 'Maybe it'll be better having a smaller part. That way you won't get too nervous on the night. You know what you're like with stage fright. At least with this part you won't have too many lines to remember.'

'There are no small parts,' Una said as she sat opposite, 'just small actors. Remember that.'

'She's right, you know.' Rachel flicked her layered hair. 'Every part is as important as the next.'

'Really?' Grace replied curtly. 'Who played the lead in *Some Like It Hot*?'

'That's easy. Marilyn Monroe.'

'And who played the waitress in the hotel?'

'Em…'

'Exactly.'

'Judi Dench was in *Shakespeare in Love* for only eight minutes, and she won an Oscar.'

'Judi Dench played the queen. Not servant number two.'

Adie gave her another squeeze, and Grace smiled ruefully.

'I'm grand, really. I'm just a bit jealous, that's all. Since Rachel's playing the lead, and Una's playing the *grandmother* of the lead.'

'Ha!' Jenny snorted from across the room, her auburn hair glowing in the sunlight. 'You're playing an oul' woman, Una? That's gas.'

'Because of my thespian skills,' Una snapped. 'It's not easy playing an old granny, you know. It takes talent.'

'Honestly, I was dreading having to watch this thing, but now I'm thinking it might be really good for a laugh.'

Jenny jumped off her perch on the window-sill, spilling a bag of sherbet and a sandwich on the floor, and picked up the *Red Riding Hood* script. Jenny's habit of eating gross lunches — she mixed chocolate and mayonnaise like they were made for each other — was a constant source of revulsion for the others.

'Tradesman number one,' Jenny mumbled now, as she read through the character list. 'Knight number three, the village fool, the king… Hang on, how come there's so many people in this? I thought *Red Riding Hood* was just Red Hiding Hood, her granny and the wolf.'

'It was,' Una said, stretching her legs nonchalantly to rest her feet on the table. 'But we had to make room for the little people.'

Rachel swatted at her while Grace sank lower into her chair.

'There are a lot more characters than usual,' Rachel said, 'because there are a lot of us doing drama. So Mr Dogberry had to put in enough parts for everybody.'

'Hence servant number two,' said Grace. She unwrapped her tin-foiled sandwiches. Egg again. She sighed and when she looked up, Delilah was on her other side, her big brown eyes smiling.

'I bet I know something that'll cheer you up,' she said. As she spoke, something began to wriggle beneath the tresses of her thick, black hair. Grace gasped as a little wood nymph – only 10 centimetres tall – burst into view, grabbing a length of Delilah's hair and swinging as if he were on a trapeze. His brown skin was grainy, like rough paper, and the scent of the woods filled the air as he twirled beneath the small girl's chin. B-brr, as Delilah had named him, had become a permanent member of their group during one of the girls' terrifying adventures in the world of witchcraft. They had been trapped on the magical island of Hy-Breasal, and it was little B-brr who had helped them escape. Now he was Delilah's constant companion.

Even so, Grace couldn't get used to seeing him hanging out of the small girl's ear or squirming under her collar. It still gave her the willies.

'We'll be with you on the night. Me and Adie,' said Delilah. 'We're doing tech. So it'll be lots of fun, don't worry.'

'Oh, yeah, I meant to say!' Adie exclaimed. 'Ms Welch was looking for volunteers from music class to help with the show. I'm doing lights, and Delilah's in charge of sound. Isn't that cool? Plus, we've to help find all the props and costumes. It's gonna be deadly.'

'There's a jumble sale in town,' Delilah said. 'Some big house is up for auction and they're selling all the contents. We're bound to find some great stuff there.'

'Yeah,' Adie said, grinning, 'we'll find you guys some awesome costumes. You're gonna look brilliant!'

'Even as servant number two?' said Grace,

smiling in spite of herself.

'Even as servant number two,' Adie said.

2

THe aLLan HouSe

Later that day Adie and Delilah stood on the grass-fringed drive and looked up at the house. It was a large Victorian townhouse of weathered red brick with a huge bay window on the ground floor. There were stripes of yellow stone under the roof and in the arches of the upper floor windows that made the place look very pretty in the sun.

The girls signed in at a table set up on the lawn, and pushed their way through the crowd in the garden, past the huge pieces of antique furniture that were drawing the most attention. The smaller stuff, they were told, was on display inside the house.

It smelled musty and damp in the hall. The wallpaper was peeling off in jagged strips and the floorboards were scuffed and stained. Adie had overheard her mum and dad discussing the family scandal in the house that had made the local newspapers. Apparently the house had been owned by a Mrs Cynthia Allan who, on her deathbed, had declared that it and all its belongings must remain forever in the family possession. Her sister-in-law had obeyed the request, though she had never lived in the house herself, so all the furniture and other items remained just as Cynthia had left them.

The family dispute had begun when the sister-in-law died, leaving everything to Cynthia's niece and nephew. The nephew vowed to abide by his aunt's wishes, but the niece had no such intentions. It was a legal battle that had gone on for some years until, finally, the courts decided that the house and contents should be sold, and the money divided between the two heirs.

'It smells weird in here,' Delilah whispered, inching down the dark hallway, feeling as if talking loudly might upset the house.

'I know,' replied Adie. 'A proper deserted house.'

She shivered as they made their way upstairs, and gently tapped the wriggling hump under Delilah's collar to remind the little nymph to behave.

'Can we just go anywhere in the house?' Delilah asked.

'I think so. They moved all the big stuff outside, but the flyer said that everything's for sale.'

Adie pushed open the first door, which creaked loudly, and coughed at the dust that filled the room. There were squares of pale, clean wood where the bed, wardrobe and other furniture had stood, but the rest of the floor was filthy. An ornate sideboard, covered in wide-eyed china dolls, stood at the far end. Most of the dolls were in a poor state, with hair straggled and thinning, and cracked porcelain faces. There were three, though, in perfect condition that looked oddly modern. One had dark red, spiky hair and piercings, another wore a long, dark fringe that covered one eye, and the third had soft, blonde curls and a flawless, white complexion.

'Weird,' said Adie.

She had a quick glance around but decided there was nothing here they could use for the show. Besides, the dolls were giving her the creeps.

In the next room, they found several small bits and pieces that could be of use. But in the third room, at the end the hallway, they hit the jackpot. It was filled floor to ceiling with piles of dresses, coats, hats, shawls and shoes. Everything looked old-fashioned, and there was a lot of lace, tweed and greying cotton.

'This is perfect,' Delilah exclaimed. 'There'll be costumes in here for everybody.'

'There's even more in here,' Adie said, swinging open the doors of a worm-eaten wardrobe. 'Let's make a pile.'

She threw a few garments into the centre of the room, then discovered a large, grey trunk tucked away in the back of the closet. Inside were the Victorian-style clothes that servants in big houses once wore – black twill dresses, white aprons and white lace caps, tailed black jackets and trousers for the men and...

'Wow. Delilah, look at this.'

It was a cap of bright, red velvet with a short brim at the front. The colour was so vibrant, it was hard to believe it had been stuffed inside a trunk all this time.

'It's gorgeous,' Delilah said.

'Should we take it?'

'Definitely. The guys will love it.'

✷✷✷

'Aaaand cue Red Riding Hood.'

Mr Dogberry pointed to centre stage. Rachel appeared.

'Your Majesty,' she said, bowing to the boy in the paper crown, 'I have no wish to abandon your coronation celebrations, but I'm afraid I must take this basket of bread to my grandmother in the woods.'

'Jenny was right,' Grace whispered to Una at the back of the Main Hall. 'This script is ludicrous.'

'Would it still be ludicrous if you were Red Riding Hood?'

'Maybe a bit less ludicrous.'

Grace folded her arms and slouched so far down into her chair that her back was nearly on the seat. She was normally at the top of her class in everything – everything except P.E., of course, and she could live with that. But since the recent revelation that she was at the very bottom of the class in drama she found herself acting less and less like the good, reliable Grace. She didn't put up her hand the moment Mr Dogberry asked a question, she didn't offer to help tidy the room when the bell went for lunch. Instead she sat at the back, slouched in her seat, mumbling complaints about how lame it all was, and how school was really boring. *This is what it must be like to be one of the bad kids,* she thought.

'Me and Rachel would be happy to give you some pointers,' Una said kindly. 'You know, so you get better at acting before the show.'

Grace slid still further into her seat.

'Are you alright, girls?' The quiet voice of Ms Lemon behind her caught Grace off guard. Ms Lemon was the French teacher, but the girls had been thrilled to discover that she was also part of a coven, and now she tutored the girls in witchcraft outside school hours. She was one of their nicest teachers, and somehow Grace felt guilty that the woman had caught her in an uncharacteristic 'I hate school' mood.

'Fine, miss,' she said, sitting up again. 'Just, you know…' she gestured vaguely at the stage, 'rehearsing for the pantomime.'

Ms Lemon smiled.

'Mr Dogberry's taking an…interesting approach to the story.'

'He's alternative, miss,' said Una.

Ms Lemon chuckled and moved towards the front. Mr Dogberry suddenly leapt from the stage, his orange-tinted spectacles almost flying off his nose, and sprinted towards Adie and Delilah as they struggled into the Main Hall carrying boxes of clothes and props.

'Splendid! The costumes!'

'My mum just brought them in, sir,' Adie said. 'It's all the stuff we got over the weekend. We spent the full budget. I hope that's okay.'

'But, of course, when you bring me such treasures!' He held out a red velvet cap and twirled it on his hand.

'Where did you find it all?' Grace asked, as she helped Delilah carry a box that was almost the same size as herself.

'We got a few things in that flea market on Dropsy Lane,' the small girl replied. 'And some things from charity shops, and then some really cool stuff from that sale in the Allan house on Sunday.'

'The Allan house?' Ms Lemon said sharply.

'Yes, miss. You know that house the brother and sister were fighting over. They sold all the stuff in it.'

'Which stuff? Which bits came from the house?'

'I'm not sure, miss,' Adie said. 'It's all mixed together now. Why? What's wrong?'

Ms Lemon took them aside while Mr Dogberry tried on a series of ill-fitting jackets.

'Mrs Allan was a witch,' she whispered. 'Vera, Meredith and I used to buy items from her before we found the magic shop in town. I don't think she was a particularly nice woman, she… It doesn't matter. But she kept enchanted objects all over the place, and you've no way of knowing what's magic and what's not. We need to get rid of anything that came from her house.'

Ms Lemon so rarely mentioned the other witches from her old coven that the girls were taken aback.

'But it's all for the show, miss,' Adie said. 'And we can't remember where everything came from.'

'I know, Adie, and I'm sorry. But this is important. You and Delilah need to pick out as many of the Allan items as you can, and get them out of here before Mr Dogberry sees them. I'll take them home and sort through them there.'

'Okay, miss.' The two girls exchanged sullen glances. All their efforts over the weekend seemed to have been a waste of time.

'I'll give you a hand,' Grace said gently. 'I'm sure there'll be plenty left that we can use.'

✳✳✳

On the edge of a cardboard box lay the cap. It wasn't bored now. There was a buzz in the room. Lots of people, nervous and excited. There was a story here, it could sense it. But it could also sense a woman that wanted to stop the fun. It slipped off the side of the box onto the floor. And there it waited, waited patiently to be found by somebody new, and for the fun to begin.

3

ROOTS in THE CARPET

'Five minutes to curtain-up. Everyone, please check your costumes.'

At the sound of Mr Dogberry's voice Grace felt instantly sick. Four lines, that's all she had to remember; four lines. But her mind had gone completely blank. She took a shallow breath and stared at her reflection in the mirror. If she was this nervous for a dress rehearsal in front of empty seats, what would happen when she had to remember her whole four lines in front of a packed Main Hall?

She pulled down the hem of the black, twill dress that was a little too short, and straightened her apron. From the heap of odds and ends in the corner, she picked a simple, white cap with a lace trim and jammed it onto her head.

'You okay?'

Rachel looked like Snow White, her pale skin complemented perfectly by the red, velvet cap she wore. Mr Dogberry had explained that in the earliest versions of *Red Riding Hood* the heroine had worn a scarlet cap, not a hooded cape, and the story had even been called Little Red Cap. When Rachel found the vibrant red hat near the costume box, she fell in love with the idea.

'Yeah. You?'

'A bit nervous. Just hope I can remember all my lines.'

Me too, thought Grace, but she pushed down her worries and followed Rachel to the stage.

✳✳✳

'Fudge!' Adie said as a lighting gel drifted to the floor like a large, pink feather.

'Are you alright up there, Adie?'

Grace stepped out of her way as the flustered girl climbed down the ladder and snatched up the gel.

'I've lost my multi-tool. You know the penknife thing that Jenny was messing with at lunchtime. I think she still has it. You wouldn't be able to get it for me, would you?'

Grace was nervous enough without the possibility of missing her cue.

'I don't know where she is,' she said unwillingly.

'She's somewhere in school. I'm so sorry to ask, but you're not on for ages, and I really need it. I can't leave the stage now, there's too much to do. Pleeeease?'

Grace smiled at Adie's pleading face. 'Sure.'

'Thank you so much.'

Grace turned, nearly tripping over Delilah as the small girl dragged a cable across the stage to a plug socket it wasn't going to reach. The girl's back looked noticeably unhunched.

'No B-brr today?' asked Grace.

'Had to leave him at home,' Delilah said. 'He's taken to chewing on wires, so I didn't dare bring him here. Mrs Quinlan's looking after him during rehearsals. She's really not happy about it.'

Grace smiled. She couldn't imagine the crotchety old witch — nicknamed Old Cat Lady, who had become Delilah's guardian — on babysitting duties for a wood nymph. She'd have given a month's pocket money to be a fly on the wall of Mrs Quinlan's kitchen for that spectacle.

Grace was hurrying past the rows of empty seats in the Main Hall when the curtain went up, the ties of her cap swinging as she ran. The first lines of the pantomime echoed from the stage and set off fresh butterflies in her stomach. She rounded the corner and was surprised to see Jenny sitting on a bench outside the Vice Principal's office.

'What are you doing here?' she asked.

'Detention.'

'What for?'

'Nothing.'

Grace raised an eyebrow and Jenny huffed in annoyance.

'You know that little ditty you learn in science class about mixing water and acid?'

'If you're doing what you oughta, add the acid to the water,' Grace said, quickly recalling the rhyme. 'It's to make sure you mix them the safe way, isn't it?'

'Yeah, I guess. Well, anyway, Cherylanne, and her friend that talks too much, couldn't remember which one you'd to add to which. So I – and I was only messing – I told them the phrase was 'if you're feeling kind of placid, add the water to the acid'. And everyone heard and went to add the water to the acid, instead of the other way around.'

'Jenny, that's terrible!'

'It's not my fault. I didn't think anyone would believe me. Anyway, someone told Mr Geiser and he gave me detention. *Detention*. It was just a joke.'

'A dangerous joke, Jenny. You could've hurt someone.'

'Don't blame me, blame physics–'

'Chemistry.'

'Whatever. It's stupid that acid explodes for no reason.'

Grace sighed and remembered why she'd gone looking for Jenny in the first place.

'Adie needs her multi-tool thing. Have you got it?'

'Yeah, sorry,' Jenny said, pulling it from her pocket. 'Forgot I had it. Hey, the show's starting. Aren't you supposed to be on stage?'

'I'm on my way.'

'Break a leg!' Grace heard Jenny call out.

✳✳✳

Grace sprinted down the side of the Main
Hall, down the corridor to the right that led
to the backstage door and… nearly hit a tree.

It was not a piece of scenery. It was an actual,
big tree. Right there in the middle of the corridor.

She took a step back, looking it up and down.
The roots seemed to go through the floor and
through the carpet, not like the material was
torn, but like the tree had grown from it. The
thick, grey trunk stretched to the ceiling. The
upper branches with their vibrant green leaves
pushed through the ceiling but, again, it looked
like they'd always been there, melded through
the square panels.

'What the…?'

In a daze, Grace stumbled past the tree, up the
three steps to the backstage door and pushed
inside. Adie smiled and held out her hand.

'Ooh, thanks!' she whispered, whipping the multi-tool from her fingers. 'You're so good.'

'Tree,' Grace said.

'Huh?'

'Tree,' she repeated, dizzy, until she felt a sharp poke in the back and she was suddenly onstage.

Rachel stood opposite in her red cap, and the king was centre-stage with a knight kneeling at his feet.

She had a line, Grace knew. This was a scene where she had a line. But which one was it?

Yes, my lord.

No, my lord.

Thank you, Madam, or

Not all the radishes could be saved, my lady, but we still have soup.

Her forehead and nose felt damp with sweat and, across the stage, the whites of Rachel's eyes grew as if the girl was trying to communicate the correct line telepathically.

'No, my lord,' Grace guessed, then slumped

with relief as the scene continued. When her cue arrived to leave the stage, she snatched Adie's hand and dragged her to the backstage door.

'What are you doing?' her friend whispered. 'I've got to change the lighting for the sword fight!'

Grace pulled her out into the corridor, where Adie's jaw dropped in shock.

'Tree,' she said, looking up.

They stood in stunned silence. Mr Graham, the Spanish teacher, arrived from the opposite direction. He stood looking up at the tree, apparently as perplexed as they were. Grace felt Adie give her a dig in the ribs. A wooden cart had appeared in front of Mr Graham; a wheelbarrow full of turnips, potatoes and other vegetables. The teacher stared at the cart for a few seconds then, as if it was the most natural thing in the world, he grabbed the handles and wheeled it back the way he had come. By the time he reached the end of the corridor he was whistling a lively tune.

'What on Earth is going on?' Adie gasped.

'I don't know,' Grace replied. 'But there's magic in this. No doubt.'

'I'm gonna get the others.'

Adie hurried through the backstage door, leaving Grace alone. She reached out and gently traced the knots in the grey bark of the weirdest tree she had ever seen.

'*Grrrr.*'

The sound was soft and low. Grace froze.

'*Grrrr.*'

There it was again.

'Hello?'

'Am gonna eat ya!'

The voice was distorted and gravelly. And it was very close. Grace started to tremble.

'Am gonna eat ya!'

'Who's there?' She crept around the tree trunk. On the other side, there was a shock of rough, brown fur.

'Am gonna eat ya… all… UP!'

41

Something big and hairy turned and leapt at her from behind the tree. Grace screamed, then took a second look, and smacked the creature hard on the shoulder.

'Andrew Wallace, you're such a *muppet*!'

Andrew stood in his wolf costume, wheezy with laughter.

'You should have seen your face! Did you think there was a real wolf in the school, Grace? Were you afraid of the Big Bad Wolf?'

He laughed some more and she pushed him away as she stomped up the steps to the door.

Andrew Wallace really was a muppet.

4

IN THE STOCKS

Daryl Kuti stood in the wings with his hands on his hips, apparently waiting for Mr Dogberry to return his crown. The drama teacher had the item perched on his head, giving instruction on the *proper* way for a king to look down on his subjects. Grace pushed past them and ran straight into Una.

'Grace, is that you?' With a curly, grey wig and milk-bottle glasses, Una looked every bit the old grandmother. She squinted her eyes and poked Grace in the cheek.

'Ow! Yes, it's me, Una. What was the poke for?'

'I was checking you were a person. Something weird is going on – I can't really see.'

'What do you mean?'

'Everything is blurry. And my hearing's gone a bit funny.'

'Your hearing's gone funny?'

'What?' Una cupped her ear.

'Are you saying you're going deaf?' shouted Grace.

'What?' Una tutted and stamped her feet. 'This is stupid. I can't hear what you're saying.'

Grace felt a twist in her stomach. The tree in the corridor, Mr Graham's vegetable cart, and now this. It was all connected.

'I've gotta go find the others. There's something very strange going on here.'

'About half an hour, I think,' Una replied.

'What? Look, never mind, just wait here.'

'*Huh?*'

'WAIT HERE!'

'Alright, alright,' Una said, wiping her nose. 'No need to yell.'

✳✳✳

Grace meant to sneak behind the stage but realised she needn't bother. The show had stopped. There was no-one on stage. She stepped forward into the spotlights that still glowed and saw people scattered throughout the Main Hall. Except it wasn't the Main Hall anymore.

In one far corner she could see the familiar painted blocks of the school walls, and an area of mud-coloured carpet, but the rest of the room had changed. It had somehow become a bustling marketplace.

There were stalls full of vegetables – Mr Graham stood shouting prices from beneath the canopy of one of them – people selling bread, meat, leather goods and even small pieces of furniture. All the students dressed as peasants now moved about the stalls haggling or selling stuff themselves. Those dressed as knights walked confidently through the masses, bragging about battles and demanding free mead.

Grace stared in awe for a few moments, then hurried across the stage, briefly stopping to straighten a jug and wipe a table clean.

Don't know why I did that, she thought.

When she found Adie and Rachel they were huddled by the soundboard.

'Are you seeing this?' Rachel said.

'And more,' Grace replied. 'It's into the corridors too. Mr Graham wasn't wearing peasant clothes, and he is now. And I saw other kids in the market that aren't in our drama class. Whatever this is, I think it's taken over the whole school.'

'Not just that. Have you tried doing any magic in the last while?'

'No. Why?' Alarmed, Grace quickly tried to originate an animal out of thin air. It was a spell she could usually do with very little effort – but try as she might, this time, no animal appeared. It was as if some force, bigger than her, was blocking her powers. She could feel it.

'Uh-oh.'

'What's happening?' Adie said, tears starting to glisten in her eyes.

'It's got to be a spell, an enchantment of some kind, or maybe… You look really nice, Adie.'

'Sorry?'

'You look really good. Like you're glowing or… I don't know, like you've got a really healthy glow.'

Rachel took an approving glance at their friend's complexion.

'You do, you know. Your skin looks great.'

'Oh,' Adie replied. 'Okay. Thanks.'

Grace shook her head.

'Anyway, we need to find Delilah and Jenny. Una's having a rough time of it. She's not just acting the part of an old woman now. She's really turning into one.'

'Ooh, bummer,' said Rachel. 'Is she getting all wrinkly?'

'No, but she's losing her sight and her hearing. We have to stop this thing, whatever it is. Where's Delilah?'

'Don't know. She was backstage earlier, but now we can't find her.'

'Damn it. Then we'll go get Jenny first. She's in detention.'

'What for?' asked Adie.

'Don't ask.'

As the girls turned to leave, a shout came from the market.

'All hail the king!'

Trumpets sounded, and Mr Dogberry, still with the crown on his head, processed into the market down a set of stone steps that led from the stage. Everyone, knights included, dropped to one knee as the teacher swept regally past, followed by the unfortunate Daryl Kuti, who was carrying the king's train.

Mr Dogberry paused in the middle of the market and his eyes swept imperiously over the crowd.

'My loyal subjects,' he called, 'I walk among you today as your king. But also as one of you — as a humble servant, a loving neighbour and a devoted friend. But mostly as your king.' Those that had been about to rise, quickly lowered themselves again and bowed their heads. 'And, as your king, I ask only for your loyalty. Your precious loyalty. And also for taxes.'

Daryl slouched around the crowd, holding out a gold-lined sack into which the peasants reluctantly dropped coins.

'I thank you for your generosity,' the king said, then turned with a swish of his ermine-lined cloak, back towards the stage.

'Quick, let's get out of here,' Grace hissed.

She pushed her friends across the boards to the backstage door. Una was beside the door leaning on a crate, and squinting.

'Come on,' said Grace, grabbing her by the elbow and hustling them all down the corridor.

'So weird,' Rachel said, twirling her red cap as she gazed at the many trees that now lined the corridor.

'In here, quick!' Grace said, hurrying to the classroom nearest the Vice Principal's office.

As they opened the door, a confused giggle escaped Adie's lips. The girls crowded in behind her and gasped in shock.

'It's not funny,' Jenny snapped.

'Of course not, I'm sorry,' said Adie. 'But what *is* it?'

Jenny's head and hands poked through a brace of timber that rested on a pole at about hip height. She was bent over at the waist, unable to pull herself free of the wooden boards that were fixed with a padlock on one side.

'They've put her in the *stocks*,' Grace said.

'Pillory,' a voice said.

Grace spun around. Behind her was a boy with blond hair in a similar predicament.

'I'm sorry?'

'It's called a pillory,' he replied. 'With stocks, the feet are locked up as well. Our feet are free,' he awkwardly raised one leg in explanation. 'So it's a pillory.'

'Are you gonna stand there all day discussing the finer points of medieval torture?' said Jenny. 'Or are you going to get us out of this and tell me what the bloody hell is going on?'

Grace examined the device. There was a wooden bolt through the brace that held it into a groove in the pole. Twisting it she managed to pull the bolt out, allowing Jenny to stand up straight. Her hands and head remained stuck in the brace, however, and she snorted.

'What about this bit?'

'It's padlocked.'

'So? Break it.'

'I'm not the freaking Hulk, Jenny.'

Jenny snorted again, slouching under the weight of the timber. It looked really uncomfortable.

The others freed the blond boy from the pole, while giving Jenny a run-down on how the Main Hall seemed to have turned into a medieval marketplace. Still in his wooden brace, the boy wandered out, as if in a daze. Grace winced as rotten fruit and vegetables came flying at him from all directions.

'Where's Ms Lemon?' Jenny asked.

'Don't know,' Grace replied. 'She may not even be in school. We don't know what time her classes finished today.'

'Then why don't we just leave. Let's just walk out of the school and find Mrs Quinlan and Ms Lemon so they can stop this.'

Grace blushed. 'I actually didn't think of that.'

Jenny turned her head awkwardly against the timber.

'Well, aren't you glad I'm here then?'

***

They couldn't leave. Where the main door should have been, there was no door; instead there was a portcullis, a thick lattice of black iron that protected the entrance of a castle. But they couldn't find a winch attached to it, and it was way too heavy to lift. The girls crept along corridors, where the school brick was sometimes visible and sometimes not. Occasionally the walls dissolved into woodland, or thatched huts, or open fields. It was weirder than weird. And still they couldn't find a single exit to the outside world. They were trapped.

'I need to sit down for a bit,' croaked Una.

'We don't have time for that, Una,' Jenny said, a little louder than she needed to.

'Oh, it's alright for you, with your young feet and your knees that work. I'm all stiff and creaky. I want some comfier shoes. And a fire… and maybe a cat.'

'Do you want to hide out somewhere, Una,' said Grace, 'while the rest of us sort this out?'

The girl with the grey curls didn't hear.

'Ooh, my bones aren't what they used to be,' she said, leaning against a wall.

This time Grace put her hand on Una's arm, made eye contact, and shouted her question.

'Suits me fine,' nodded Una. 'But I want somewhere comfortable to sit.'

'We'll find somewhere suitable.'

'Somewhere that's not got any damp.'

'We'll do our best.'

'And I want a hot water bottle.'

'We haven't got a hot water bottle.'

'Meany.'

5

THUNDER and LIGHTNING

After depositing Una in a storeroom that was well on its way to becoming a small, thatched cottage, the girls headed back to the Main Hall. The corridor from the A block was now unrecognisable. There was no brick wall or school carpet anywhere, just a rough, grassy path with cartwheel tracks, and what seemed like sky above them and fresh air all around them. Grace thought that heading into one of the adjacent fields would eventually lead them to the real outside but, after walking for some time, they just circled back to where they started. The enchantment was making sure they remained in the school.

Across the fields, Grace spotted a small, sodden creature running towards them.

'Delilah!' she called. She'd never seen the tiny girl looking so haggard and distressed. Her hair and clothes were soaked, her eyes red and puffy, and she was shaking all over.

'What's going on?' Delilah cried.

'We don't know, but we're going to figure it out. Are you okay?'

'It's been raining. It's been raining down on me everywhere I go and…and…thunder! Thunder and lightning. And I was all on my own.'

'It's alright,' Adie soothed. 'You've found us now. You're safe.'

'I didn't hear any thunder,' said Jenny.

'There was!' Delilah's voice rose. 'There was loads of it. Loads!'

At that moment, there was a terrific flash of lightning and a second later a rolling groan of thunder.

'See?' Delilah said, cowering with her face in her hands. 'It's all the time.'

'Hang on,' Jenny said, the wooden pillory turning as she twisted to face the small girl. 'Are you afraid of thunder?'

'A little bit. Yes.'

'Okay, then I think another one's coming.'

'Jenny,' Grace said sharply.

'No, no, listen.' Jenny leaned down to Delilah as far as the brace would allow. 'There's more thunder and lightning coming. Can you hear it? Right now!'

The small girl moaned and then gasped as a fork of lightning struck the track ahead and growling thunder shook the ground beneath their feet. Delilah started to cry.

'What are you doing?' Grace snapped. 'She

just told you she doesn't like thunder. Why are you making it worse?'

'I'm not,' Jenny replied. '*She* is. Sorry, Delilah, I just needed to see if I was right. And I think I am. Every time you get upset, there's thunder and lightning. *You're* causing the storm.'

Grace thought for a moment.

'Sound,' she said, clicking her fingers. 'Delilah, you were in charge of the sound effects, weren't you – the lightning, and all the weather stuff. So now you're…the weather, I guess. Then that means…oh, no…Adie, no, no, no!'

Adie's complexion was now more than glowing. It was positively radiant. Grace reached out a hand and touched her cheek.

'It's not just light,' she said. 'You're warm too.'

'What are you talking about?' Adie seemed oblivious to the rays of light that were streaming from her skin.

'You were in charge of lighting. You're the

light. I mean, you're becoming…'

'What? The sun? Are you telling me I'm turning into the *sun*?'

Grace wanted to hug her friend whose eyes were wide with terror, but she was afraid she might get burned.

'I think so.'

Adie raised her hands. They glimmered with yellow luminescence.

'The longer it goes on, the worse it gets,' Grace said. 'We need to find out what's causing this. Now.'

There was a cracking of clouds and a sudden downpour. Delilah looked up through the rain with her big, brown eyes.

'Sorry.'

✳✳✳

'There's one computer left. Look, over there, in the far corner.'

Inside what had once been one of the computer rooms, Adie pointed to the last remaining

PC. The girls climbed over twisting vines and bushes of stinging nettles to crowd around the screen that looked utterly out of place.

'Rachel, you're up,' said Grace.

Rachel sat down, pushing her red cap back on her head, and began typing furiously.

'Alrighty,' she said after a while, 'we could be looking at a hex.'

'Like a curse?'

'Yeah, another witch or magic person taking revenge.'

'But wouldn't that happen instantly?' Jenny asked. 'Adie's not totally turned yet, and we're still aware of what's going on. A hex wouldn't happen gradually, would it?'

'Probably not. In that case, maybe a conjured spirit? Something medieval that's trying to recreate its old world?'

'Don't think so,' said Grace. 'The peasant clothes aren't authentic. And the way the king collected taxes in person? That would never happen. This isn't a genuine medieval world we're in.'

'Nerd alert,' said Jenny.

'Shut up.'

'Hmm,' Rachel said, doing another search. 'Ooh, anyone want to know what happens in the next episode of *Sunset Lives*?'

'No,' Jenny growled. 'Get on with it.'

'Alright, calm down. I was only asking. Okay, I think it's got to be an enchantment of some kind.'

'But who would do that?' Adie said. 'And why?'

'Maybe it's an old one,' said Delilah. She had gathered herself and was looking much calmer.

'How do you mean?'

'It could have been an enchantment done years ago, decades, and something's set it off again.'

'But how is an enchantment able to hang around without the witch that cast it?' said Grace.

'If it's sealed inside an object and the spell is really strong. If the object doesn't get damaged, or broken, or burnt, the enchantment can survive in there for ages.'

'The Allan house!' Adie exclaimed. 'All that stuff Ms Lemon took off us. We must have missed…oh dear.'

She gently pulled the red cap from Rachel's head and held the brim between thumb and forefinger.

'Oh my God!' Jenny said. 'How did we not think of that straight away? We're idiots. We're all idiots.'

'Stop that,' said Grace. 'We've had a lot on our minds. At least we've figured it out now. I mean–'

Suddenly Rachel squealed as the computer disappeared and was replaced by a foul-smelling plant with giant purple flowers that dripped sticky goo.

'Fudge!' said Grace. 'Now how are we going to figure out how to get the enchantment out?'

'Can't we just burn the cap?' said Jenny. 'Like Delilah said.'

'Not while it's actually doing magic,' the small girl replied. 'That would only work if it was dormant.'

'Great.'

'What about Ms Lemon's room? I know she keeps a few charms and things in there. She might have a few books in the storeroom too.'

✳✳✳

Ms Lemon's room was in the C block, and was one of the few places in the school that still looked like the school. Jenny sat down, parking her pillory on the desk in front, and sighing with relief.

'You have no idea how heavy this thing is. Seriously, I deserve a medal.'

'I don't know,' Grace said, as she flicked through one of the tattered books the girls had found in the adjacent storeroom, 'maybe you're getting your just desserts for nearly blowing up your class.'

'If I wasn't so tired and sore right now, I'd stand up and–'

'And what?'

'Yell at you, that's what. You'd get a good yelling at.'

'Good thing you're in the pillory, then.'

'Zip it, Brennan.'

'Found it!' Rachel held her hand in the air and grinned. 'I've got it, right here. Evacuation of Enchanted Objects.'

She laid the book on the teacher's desk and began skimming down the pages.

'It looks like there are several options available. One requires the blood of an ox – ew – and one of his legs.'

'I'm not killing an ox,' said Adie.

Grace shielded her eyes as she tried to look at her friend.

'We don't have an ox.'

'Well, I wouldn't kill it if we did have one.'

'Me neither. Next option.'

'Ewww!' Rachel grimaced as she flipped the page. 'That's…that's even worse. No, we're not doing that.'

'Which one *can* we do,' Jenny said impatiently. 'Just skip to that one.'

'Maybe this last one, but there's loads of ingredients.' She ran her finger down the page. 'The copper wire and iron shavings we can get from the metalwork room. Some of this other stuff we can get in the science labs, I'm sure. A moth orchid?'

'Mr Fleur has one of those on his windowsill,' Delilah said. 'It might still be there.'

'Cool. Then there's just, ooh… ah, now, this is our problem.'

'What?' said Grace.

'The hair of a varg.'

'What's a varg?'

'That's the problem. I haven't a clue. Does anyone else?'

Grace felt a sprinkling of raindrops that steadily grew in size and speed, soaking through the white cotton of her servant's hat.

'Delilah knows.'

The small girl sat cross-legged on a desk, her eyebrows nearly touching, her brow had furrowed so much.

'A wolf,' she whispered. 'It means wolf.'

'Where the hell are we going to find a wolf in school?' said Jenny, laboriously raising her pillory from the desk.

'Andrew Wallace,' said Grace. 'The big, bad wolf.'

'But he's not an actual wolf.'

Grace remembered her earlier encounter with Andrew and shrugged. 'If he's not yet, he will be soon.'

6

THE big, bad woLF

The sight of the marketplace made Grace feel
queasy. There was nothing left of the school
there now. Even the stage was gone. In its
place stood a timber platform scattered with
huge wooden blocks and, in the centre, a gallows with a hangman's noose. She gulped.
When Delilah noticed the rope, there was a
huge clap of thunder.

'We'd better hurry,' she said, 'before all the
science labs and the metalwork room are gone

for good.'

The mood in the market had definitely changed. There was no more light-hearted banter from the stalls. Now people stood hunched over their wares, careful not to make eye contact with the palace guards that patrolled the pathways. Grace saw one guard take a swipe at a boy that didn't get out of her way quick enough.

'Delilah's right. We'll have to split up. Head for the rooms farthest from here – they should be the ones that still have school stuff in them.'

Squish.

A slushy, overripe tomato hit Jenny's cheek and slid down her face in a gloopy mess.

'I am done with this,' she said. 'I am very, very done with this.'

Splat.

Another piece of rotten fruit. This one hit her hard on the head. Then more, and more. She ducked as best she could with her head and arms trapped in the pillory.

'Thief!' someone yelled in the crowd.

'What? I'm no thief!'

'Thief! Thief! Thief!'

Before the girls could stop it, two palace guards had grabbed hold of Jenny and wrestled her to the floor.

'Well, well, well,' one of them snickered. 'How did you get free? Not to worry. We'll put you back on display, where you're supposed to be, and these people can take a proper shot at you. The king is clamping down on crooks like you. No more mercy.'

There was a cheer from the crowd. Grace ran at one of the guards and tried to tackle him, but he barely noticed as she thumped uselessly on his armour.

'Just go!' Jenny shouted to the girls. 'Get the stuff and stop the enchantment! I'll be alright.'

Thunder and lightning raged overhead as the mob dragged Jenny away. Grace could hardly believe what was happening and Adie started sobbing. The girls stood drenched in

Delilah's storm, paralysed with fear that the gallows might be put to use.

It was Rachel who snapped them out of it. She rapidly issued instructions to each of the friends. Although Grace was in a daze, she understood her role. She was to head to the metalwork room, while the others spread out throughout the school. She took off without a word and ran like her life depended on it.

She sprinted through thick woodland, cursing under her breath each time she tripped on the curling roots and twisted vegetation. Finally she reached the P block and almost cried out in relief as her feet touched carpet rather than grass.

There were still two classrooms left, and one of them was the metalwork room. Still warm from the welder and other machines that had been used that day, the room was empty of people but full of equipment. There were scraps of metal and plastic scattered across the tables, and shavings littered the floor.

Against one wall were dozens of drawers filled with rivets, blades, nuts and bolts. They made an awful racket as Grace snapped them open and shut, but it didn't matter, because halfway through the middle set of drawers she found what she needed: spools of copper wire. Then, using a dustpan and brush, she swept up a panful of metal shavings from the floor. She couldn't tell which metal was which, but reckoned there was bound to be iron in the pile of scraps she had collected.

She now had everything she had come for – and just in time too, because as she went through the door, it groaned and twisted into a knotty sycamore tree. Behind her, the walls of the metalwork room were sprouting into leafy woodland. But above the sound of leaf bursting through brick was another sound…

'*Grrrr.*'

Grace froze, and sucked in a breath. The sound was familiar.

'*Grrrr.*'

Grace flattened herself against the sycamore. Maybe he hadn't seen her. Maybe he didn't know she was there…

No such luck.

'Am gonna eat ya!'

The creature did not bother to hide this time. His furry silhouette, much larger than before, slouched through the trees, his watchful eyes fixed on Grace. He walked on all fours, but as he crept closer he reared up on his hind legs.

'Am gonna eat ya!'

Grace whimpered. He wasn't Andrew Wallace anymore. His freckled skin was hairy and dark, his snub nose had elongated, and his blue eyes burned bright and yellow. Andrew had really become a big, bad wolf.

'Andrew,' Grace hoped she could still reach the boy inside. 'You're not yourself. Haven't you noticed how you've changed? Your nose is black and covered in hair.'

'All the better to smell you with!'

She wished she had a mirror to show him.

'And your eyes, they're not human.'

'All the better to see you with!'

'And your teeth…' Her voice faded as she watched his dripping canines.

'All the better to EAT you with!'

The wolf lunged. Grace whirled behind the sycamore, tipping the metal shavings into her hand at the same moment. With the dustpan empty, she leapt from behind the tree trunk swinging it as hard as she could. The pan hit the wolf across the face with a loud smack. He tumbled into a clump of bushes, snarling and growling. Grace turned and ran as fast as her legs could carry her.

He didn't follow. Slowing to a jog as she passed the marketplace on her way to the last remaining science lab, she realised she needed a handful of his fur for the spell.

No way, she thought to herself. *You might be brave sometimes, but you're not a fool.*

She'd have to go back and collect the hair

when she had backup from the others.

'Halt!' A knight stood in front Grace, her chain-mailed hand held out. 'You, servant girl, I am thirsty. Fetch me some mead.'

'I'm in a hurry.'

Grace pushed past her and the knight grabbed her arm. A deep, red ponytail hung from the back of her helmet and, through the knightly visor, Grace recognised the dark, soulless eyes of Tracy Murphy, also known as the Beast.

'Oh, fudge,' Grace groaned.

Tracy was the school bully, built like a tank and likely to run anyone over who didn't do exactly what she said.

'No, no, not fudge! I want *mead*,' the large girl snapped. 'I am not hungry, but thirsty. Fetch me some. And make it quick.'

Two helmeted knights appeared either side of Tracy, and Grace could only assume they were her loyal henchmen, Trish and Bev. All three wore swords at their sides and looked huge in their suits of armour. Telling them all to get lost was not an option.

'But of course, sir knight,' Grace dropped a deep curtsy. 'I shall fetch your mead and return forthwith.'

She turned to leave, and Tracy gripped her arm again.

'That road leads to the farms. The ale houses are this way.'

Fudge, Grace thought. *There's nothing for it now.*

'You are correct, sir knight.'

She smiled and turned towards the marketplace. She walked a few paces, and then dropped to the ground and scurried away between Trish's feet. Bev screeched and ploughed into Trish in an effort to catch her. The two knights tumbled into the grass in a clanging cacophony of metal plate. Grace heard the roaring commands of Tracy in the background, but didn't stop running until she had made it safely to the science lab.

✳✳✳

'There you are,' Rachel said when Grace came panting through the door. 'What took you so long?'

'Wolf,' Grace gasped, 'and the Beast, and the henchmen.'

'Hmm, been quite busy, haven't we? Didn't happen to get a clump of hair from the wolf, did you?'

Grace shot her a look as she struggled to catch her breath.

'No, no, of course not.' Rachel held her hands up. 'Don't worry, we'll go after him together when we've got everything else ready.'

'Are you okay?' came a soft voice behind Grace, who turned, smiling, to face Adie.

'Ow! Adie!' She clapped her hands over her eyes. The light shining from her friend was now too strong. 'God, you're getting brighter all the time!'

'I know, I'm sorry. I try to turn it down, but

nothing seems to work.'

Grace turned away and opened her eyes, but coloured shapes danced in her vision.

'We'll have to be careful. You could really blind one of us.'

'Should I go wait in the store cupboard?'

'Oh, Adie, I didn't mean that, I just meant…'

Grace trailed off, but the uncomfortable truth was that having Adie out of sight was a good idea.

'It's okay,' said Adie. 'I'll be in the cupboard.'

Grace felt a pang of guilt when she heard the storeroom door click closed.

'Ouch. Poor Adie,' said Rachel, fiddling with a bunsen burner.

'Do you have a better idea?'

'No.'

'Then let's get on with this, and get her and everything else back to normal.'

7

magic in the science Lab

The stuff bubbling away in the round-bottomed flask smelled really gross. Grace couldn't tell which ingredient was causing the stench, but she had to breathe through her mouth to block it out.

The flask sat above the bunsen burner on one of the desks in the science lab, held in place with a clamp attached to an iron stand.

The girls felt rather proud that they'd adapted the book's instructions so well to the scientific environment.

'Nearly done,' Delilah said, holding her nose and giving the green liquid another stir.

With the small girl so focussed on the potion, there hadn't been a drop of rain for ages. Rachel sighed and wiped her brow.

'So what's the plan to get–'

She never finished her sentence.

'*RAAAAAAAAAGH!!*'

A roar shook the walls – the roar of a wild, hungry animal. The savagery of it was terrifying. As the door exploded inwards, sending splinters flying in all directions, the shocked girls recoiled in horror.

A monster, a dark, hairy wolf from a nightmare, ploughed into the room.

Grace managed to swipe the flask before the creature crashed into the lab desk. Made of solid wood and fixed to the floor, the lab desk crumpled as if it was matchsticks. There was an explosion of thunder and lightning as Delilah screamed and sprinted into a corner.

'His hair!' screamed Grace. 'Grab a clump of his hair!'

'Are you crazy?' Rachel wailed from the other side of the room. 'How do we do that?'

Grace cowered behind a desk, watching the yellow eyes scan the room.

He'll go for Rachel, she thought suddenly. *Red Riding Hood.*

Rachel clutched the red velvet cap in one hand and, sure enough, the wolf spotted it. He hunkered to the floor, ready to spring.

'Rachel!' Grace yelled. 'Watch out!'

The wolf leapt. Rachel vaulted over one desk, then another, only a few centimetres ahead of his snapping jaws. He followed her, sometimes leaping a desk, sometimes smashing through it.

Grace looked desperately to Delilah. 'Lightning, Delilah! Now!'

The small girl nodded, clamped her hands

over her ears and cried out. There was a massive crack of thunder and, at the same instant, an orange fork of lightning struck the floor between Rachel and the wolf. The wolf fell back in shock, and Grace could smell singed fur. He quickly got to his feet.

'Another one! Quick!'

But the wolf heard and a look of cunning came into his eyes. He reared back on his hind legs, and shoved the splintered remains of a desk towards Delilah's corner. The pile of wood shot forward, and the small girl was buried beneath it.

'Delilah, no!'

Rachel and Grace faced the wolf. His breath was quick, and saliva dripped from his open jaws. He was much more a wolf now than human, but Grace could swear he was smiling.

'Cover your eyes!' called a voice from the storeroom. 'I'm coming out!'

Grace immediately covered her face with

her free hand, but Adie's light was now so awe-some that it even pierced the gaps between her fingers. She gasped and squeezed her eyes tight shut.

The wolf had no idea what was coming. He howled in fear against the searing brightness. But then came another sound. A yelp of pain. Seconds later Grace felt an extremely hot hand add something to the flask she was clutching.

'Get somewhere safe! Destroy the cap!' Adie shouted.

'But what about you?'

'Go! I'll keep him covered!'

Grace nodded, still with her eyes shut, and felt her way out of the room. Rachel made it outside and together they sprinted for the woods by the marketplace.

There was now a huge fight going on between the knights and the stallholders. Grace could hear Tracy's voice among them, and wondered if the Beast was taking her anger out on the unsuspecting peasants.

'We need a flame,' Rachel whispered, as they crept past the commotion, 'to finish the mixing.'

Grace spied a lantern hanging from a candle stall and snatched it.

A few metres into the woods they knelt down, lifting the metal casing off the lantern and holding the flask over the candle. After a minute or so, the liquid started to bubble and the foul stench returned.

'That should do it,' said Rachel.

The lovely red cap lay on the woodland floor. Grace poured a small stream of the green potion over it and waited.

Nothing happened.

They waited some more.

Still nothing.

'Why isn't it working?' asked Rachel.

'I don't know. How long did the book say it would take?'

'It didn't, but I presumed it would be quicker than this.'

They waited another minute. They were still surrounded by trees – and angry voices from the marketplace were coming closer.

'It's not the right thing,' Grace said, sobs of frustration choking her. She looked up at Rachel and there were tears in her eyes. 'That's not the enchanted object. It must be something else. But it could be anything. What are we going to do?'

'Well, look who it is.' The fierce armoured shape of Tracy Murphy was silhouetted by the light from the marketplace. 'You owe me a tankard of mead, servant girl.'

'I don't have any mead.'

'Then that's too bad for you.'

Tracy's fist swung out and Grace rolled to avoid it. She whimpered as she landed on the candle and smelled her own hair singe. She quickly patted down her hair but some leaves near the candle had caught fire, and she crawled quickly away from the heat. Meanwhile, Rachel, who had leapt onto Tracy's back, was being dragged off by the henchmen.

'Take the flask and run!' Rachel shouted.

'Run where? There's nowhere to go.'

'Just *run*, Grace!'

Grace grabbed the flask – then paused. Something had caught her eye.

'Grace! What are you waiting for?'

Grace was staring at her white cap, which had fallen off her head. It now lay on the ground where she had rolled over the candle, right in the middle of the rising flames. And yet it wasn't burning. It sat right in the middle of the fire and didn't burn. The plain old white cotton cap that had come from the house of Mrs Cynthia Allan.

She felt the Beast's hand grip her collar, but Grace was on a mission now. She fired an elbow backwards and caught Tracy on the chin, right under her helmet. There was a gurgle and Grace felt her collar come free. She plunged her hand between flickering flames, squealing in pain, and snatched her cap.

She poured the remaining contents of the flask over the white material. For one horrible moment she thought she had made a mistake, but then the green stain on the cotton fizzled and smoked. The cap trembled for a moment, and then burst into flames. Within seconds there were only flaky pieces of ash left.

The nightmare fairytale world started to melt away. Grace watched reality sweep back into the school, a fizzling wave that revealed painted brick walls and halls of mud-coloured carpet. The square panels of the ceiling pushed through the blue sky, and the trees sank and shrivelled into nothing. Her shoulders ached as they relaxed, and she breathed in deeply.

It felt as if she were waking from a dream. Behind her, Tracy Murphy sat slouched against the wall, rubbing her head and groaning.

In the Main Hall, students dressed in uniform and others in peasant costume, looked around as if they had all been about to do something, but couldn't remember what it was. Slowly the crowd dispersed, and Grace could see that Rachel had disentangled herself from Trish and Bev, who now stood arguing over who had wrecked whose hairdo.

Back in the science lab they found an unradiant Adie unburying Delilah from her corner of the room. The small girl emerged bruised but smiling, with no trace of a thundercloud in sight. The desks that had been smashed lay in smithereens and, in the middle of them, sat Andrew Wallace in his now somewhat tattered wolf costume. He glanced up sheepishly, his face bright red, and Grace wondered if he had some inkling that he was to blame for the mess.

If he did realise, he didn't stick around to explain or apologise. Without offering to help clear up, he high-tailed it out of there before any teachers showed up.

'Nice. I think I preferred him when he was a wolf,' said Grace.

'Do you remember everything?' asked Adie.

'Yeah, but…actually, no. It's disappearing, like a dream, you know? You remember it when you first wake up, but then it starts drifting away. Are you getting that?'

'Yeah. Still remember where we left Una though. Let's go get her before we forget.'

'And Jenny along the way. She's bound to be in a better mood now she's out of that pillory thing.'

✳✳✳

Una slumped on an upturned bucket in the A block storeroom, head back against the wall, eyes closed, legs resting on a shelf. A thin stream of drool dripped from the corner of her mouth. She was snoring lightly.

'Charming,' said Jenny.

'Huh?' Una woke and sat up, her eyes

squinting against the light from the A block. She blinked at her friends who stood squeezed in the doorway, and rolled back her shoulders.

'Hey! I feel okay! My bones aren't hurting. And I can hear. Yis sorted it!' Una looked at her watch. 'Took you long enough.'

'You're welcome, Grandma. It wasn't easy,' said Grace. She screwed up her eyes in concentration. 'We had to...there was a wolf, and something about a market...and a cap...?'

The others murmured agreement and disagreement.

'Sounds fascinating,' Una said, climbing to her feet and fixing her wig and milk-bottle glasses. 'That's a bestseller you've got there. Don't forget to write that one down.'

'You're hilarious.'

'I thank you. Lunch anyone?'

'It's really late,' said Adie.

'Okay. Dinner anyone?'

'Yeah, I'm starving,' said Jenny.

Una threw an arm around Jenny's shoulders and turned to go. Grace and the girls followed them up the A block corridor that was no longer full of ... what had it been? Trees?

Ah, maybe, maybe not. It didn't seem to matter anymore.

OTHER books FROM

erika mcGann

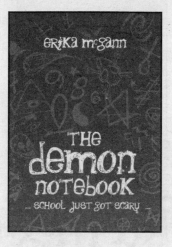

THE demon noTebooK

Grace and her four best friends, Jenny, Rachel, Adie and Una, are failed witches – and they have a notebook full of useless spells to prove it. But one night, they stumble upon real magical powers – and their notebook takes on a diabolical life of its own. The girls watch, helpless, as, one by one, their spells start to work, moving relentlessly towards the worst one of all …

Can Grace and her friends stem the wave of powerful magic … before tragedy strikes?

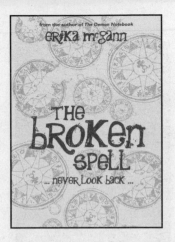

from the author of *The Demon Notebook*

erika mcgann

THE bROKEn SPELL

... never look back ...

THE bROKEn SPeLL

Trainee witch Grace and her four best friends love to have fun with their spells. So when the dazzling Ms Gold comes along offering to help the talented young coven, they jump at the chance. Before long they are becoming blonde bombshells, creating cute pets out of thin air, not to mention taking fabulous flying lessons!

But the daring friends make a magical mistake that drags the past into the present. Suddenly Grace has to work out who she can really trust...

THE WATCHING WOOD

When Grace and her friends are forced to take part in the Witch Trials, they risk life and limb to compete against other trainee witches in magical, death-defying stunts.

But when they end up in the middle of an ancient and bloody feud, Grace must outwit powerful witches, avoid the clutches of menacing faeries, and bring her friends back together. But have the girls enough power between them to make it back home?